Rabbit & Robot
and RIBBIT

Rabbit & Robot
and RIBBIT

Cece Bell

CANDLEWICK PRESS

For my great friends and co-conspirators,
Sarah Ketchersid and Heather McGee

Candlewick Sparks®. Candlewick Sparks is a registered
trademark of Candlewick Press, Inc.

First paperback edition 2017

Library of Congress Catalog Card Number 2015940265
ISBN 978-0-7636-7935-4 (hardcover)
ISBN 978-0-7636-9782-2 (paperback)

18 19 20 21 22 TLF 10 9 8 7 6 5 4 3 2

Printed in Dongguan, Guangdong, China

This book was typeset in Scala and Digital.
The illustrations were created digitally.

Candlewick Press
99 Dover Street
Somerville, Massachusetts 02144

visit us at www.candlewick.com

CONTENTS

CHAPTER ONE
Ribbit

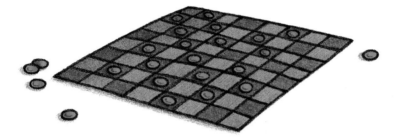

Rabbit stood at Robot's front door.

"Robot does not know that I am here," said Rabbit. "I will surprise him!"

Rabbit rang the doorbell.

Ding dong!

Robot opened the door.

"Surprise!" yelled Rabbit.

"Hello, Rabbit," said Robot. "I was
not expecting you."

"Were you surprised?" asked Rabbit.

"Yes," answered Robot. "Please
come in."

"Thanks," said Rabbit. "What's up?"

"I am playing checkers," said Robot.

"I *love* checkers," said Rabbit. "Let's play!"

"Um," said Robot. "I am already engrossed in a game—"

"Engrossed?" said Rabbit. *"Gross!"*

"I will say that in a different way,"
said Robot. "I am *very interested* in a
game already." He pointed to a small
frog sitting next to the checkerboard.
"Rabbit, this is Ribbit."

"Ribbit," said Ribbit.

"Oh! Um . . . hi," said Rabbit.

"Ribbit," said Ribbit.

"Um . . . *yeah,*" said Rabbit.

"Ribbit and I are going to finish our game," said Robot. "You can watch."

"*Hmph,*" muttered Rabbit.

Robot and Ribbit began to play. Rabbit watched.

"Ribbit," said Ribbit.

"Hee hee," giggled Robot. "Ha ha hee!"

"What's so funny?" asked Rabbit.

"Ribbit is humorous," said Robot.

"Oh, *really?*" said Rabbit. "All I heard was *ribbit*. That isn't funny at all!"

"Ribbit told a joke," explained Robot. "My Built-in Frog Glossary can show you what Ribbit just said."

Robot pushed a button on his front. A long slip of paper came out of a slot. Rabbit read it.

"Are you *kidding* me?" cried Rabbit. "You got *all these words* from just one *ribbit*?"

"Yes," said Robot.

"Ribbit," said Ribbit.

"Hee hee," giggled Robot.

"Good grief!" fussed Rabbit. "I don't have time for this. I have stuff to do. I have a *whole list* of stuff to do! I'm going home."

"I think you should stay," said Robot.

"*Hmph,*" muttered Rabbit.

"Ribbit and I are planning to watch TV," said Robot.

Rabbit's ears perked up. "Really? When?"

"After we finish our game," said Robot.

"What show?" asked Rabbit.

"*Cowboy Jack Rabbit,*" answered Robot. "It is Ribbit's favorite show."

"*Cowboy Jack Rabbit?* That's *my* favorite show, too!" cried Rabbit.

"I know," said Robot. "I forgot to inform you about our plan. I was engrossed in the game."

"*Gross,*" said Rabbit. "Um . . . I think I'll stay after all."

"Wonderful," said Robot.

"Ribbit," said Ribbit.

"Ha ha hee," chuckled Robot.

"Aw, finish your game already!" said Rabbit.

CHAPTER TWO

RIBBIT

Rabbit and Robot and Ribbit watched *Cowboy Jack Rabbit* on TV.

"Um," said Rabbit. "What are those little black things in the popcorn?"

"Flies," answered Robot. "Ribbit loves flies. In fact, Ribbit is *engrossed* in them."

"Gross!" hollered Rabbit.

"My Good Manners Meter says:
Make food that your guests will enjoy,"
said Robot. "That is why I added flies to
the popcorn."

"What about *me?*" snapped Rabbit.
"I don't see any carrots in the popcorn."

"I apologize," said Robot. "I did not
know that you would be here."

"*Hmph,*" muttered Rabbit. "I didn't
know that *someone else* would be here."

Robot spat out a slip of paper. He read it. "Aha," said Robot. "My Emotion Decoder reports that you are . . ."

"*Jealous!?*" cried Rabbit.

"Yes, jealous," said Robot. "But you should not be. I am a friend to Ribbit. I am a friend to you. Perhaps *you* can be a friend to Ribbit, too."

"No thanks," said Rabbit. "Anyone who eats flies is *gross.*"

"Ribbit," said Ribbit sadly.

Robot spat out more paper. "Oh, dear," said Robot. "Did you understand what Ribbit said?"

"NO!" barked Rabbit. "Because all Ribbit ever says is RIBBIT!"

"Ribbit is sad," said Robot. "Ribbit says that she would like to be *your* friend."

"SHE!?" cried Rabbit.

"She also says that you are cute," said Robot.

"Say *what*?" said Rabbit.

CHAPTER THREE
RIBBIT

Robot turned off the TV. "That was wonderful," he said. "I loved when Cowboy Jack Rabbit said, '*This town ain't big enough for the both of us!*'"

"I missed that part," said Rabbit. "I wasn't *engrossed* in the show. *Someone* kept staring at me."

"Ribbit," said Ribbit.

Robot laughed. "Ribbit is humorous. She said 'gross'—just like you do."

"I guess that *is* kind of funny," agreed Rabbit. "So . . . what should we do next?"

"Ribbit!" said Ribbit.

"I *still* can't understand that frog," said Rabbit. "What did she say?"

"Ribbit said that she would like to play Cowboy Jack Rabbit," answered Robot.

"That's a great idea!" said Rabbit.

Rabbit found a cowboy hat in Robot's costume box. "And I'll be Cowboy Jack Rabbit!"

Ribbit's tongue zapped the hat out of
Rabbit's paws. "Ribbit!" she barked.
"Ribbit says *no*," said Robot.

"*I see!*" snapped Rabbit. "Why not?"
"Ribbit," said Ribbit.
"Ribbit says that *she* wants to be
Cowboy Jack Rabbit," explained Robot.

Rabbit snatched the hat back. "Cowboy Jack Rabbit is a boy rabbit. He is *not* a girl frog," said Rabbit smugly. "I am a boy. I am a rabbit. Therefore, *I* should be Cowboy Jack Rabbit."

"Ribbit," croaked Ribbit. She zapped the hat back. "RIBBIT!"

"Oh yeah?" said Rabbit. "Well, ribbit ribbit RIBBBBBBIT!"

Ribbit stuck out her tongue. Rabbit grabbed it. "This town ain't big enough for the both of us!" he yelled.

Robot turned up his Volume Knob.

Rabbit and Ribbit stopped. They looked at Robot. Slips of paper shot out of his slots. More slips of paper covered the floor. The slips of paper kept coming and coming.

"You look a little pink, Robot," said Rabbit. "Are you OK?"

"My Emotion Decoder is getting hot," said Robot. "You are both showing many emotions. The Decoder cannot keep up. I think I need to—"

CHAPTER FOUR

Ribbit

THUNK.

"Oh, no," moaned Rabbit.

"Ribbit," sniffled Ribbit.

"Ribbit!?" cried Rabbit. "Is that all you can say at a time like this?"

Rabbit began running around Robot's house. "We need to find Robot's Owner's Manual!" he shouted.

Ribbit stayed near Robot. She looked closely at his buttons and slots.

Rabbit ran over to Robot's coatrack and shook it. "No Owner's Manual here!" he shouted.

"Riddit," said Ribbit.

"I can't understand you!" shouted Rabbit. He ran over to Robot's checkerboard and kicked it. "No Owner's Manual here, either!"

"Riddit!" croaked Ribbit.

"I heard you the first time!" yelled
Rabbit. He ran over to the popcorn
bowl and flipped it over.

"Still nothing! Just a bunch of coats!
And checkers! And dead flies! And a
frog who refuses to help!"

Rabbit kept running. He shook and
kicked and flipped everything in sight.

Ribbit shot out her tongue. Rabbit tripped over it. He fell to the ground.

"Ow!" cried Rabbit. "What did you do *that* for?"

Ribbit pointed to one of Robot's buttons. "REEDIT," she croaked.

"I *still* don't understand what you're saying." Rabbit sighed. He looked carefully at Robot's buttons.

"Oh!" he gasped. "Words! Were you saying 'Read it'?"

"Read it!" cried Ribbit.

Rabbit read it.

Rabbit pushed the button four times.

Robot shook and shuddered.

"He's waking up!" shouted Rabbit. "Give me a hug, Ribbit!"

Robot's eyes snapped open.

"Heh heh," chuckled Rabbit. He let go of Ribbit.

"How did you revive me?" asked Robot.

"Ribbit figured it out," answered Rabbit. "She looked closely at your buttons and slots. In fact, she was *engrossed* in them."

"Gross," said Robot.

"Hee hee," giggled Rabbit. "Ribbit saw some words on a button," he explained. "She said 'Read it'—and I did!"

"I am glad you listened," said Robot. "Thank you both for your help."

"You're welcome," said Rabbit. He smiled at Ribbit. "I am sorry, Ribbit. Robot was right. I was jealous."

"Ribbit," said Ribbit.

"She said she's sorry too, didn't she?" asked Rabbit.

"You are correct," said Robot. "She also wants to try playing Cowboy Jack Rabbit again."

"Yeah!" said Rabbit. "I know! I'll be Cowboy Jack Rabbit. Robot can be Cowboy Jack Robot. And Ribbit, *you* can be Cowboy Jack *Ribbit*!"

Rabbit put the hat on Ribbit's head. Ribbit smiled.

"Rabbit," said Ribbit. She gave
Rabbit a little kiss.

"Hee hee!" giggled Robot.

"Hmph," muttered Rabbit.